To:
From:

Sweet Dreams

A Goodnight Lullaby

words by Lillian Jaine
pictures by Marybeth Nelson

sourcebooks wonderland

It's time for bed on Sesame Street,
but Elmo just can't get to sleep!

He's counted sheep from one to ten,
and then back down to one again.
But still he sits with open eyes
and looks out at the starry skies.

So now let's sing a special song
to help him sleep the whole night long!

Good night, sleep tight.

Don't let Twiddlebugs
steal the blanket tonight!

TWIDDLE BUGS WELCOME!

End the day with a bedtime treat,
something tasty, something sweet!

Take a bath with your favorite toy,
with bubbles that you'll both enjoy!

SOAP

SOAP

Now you're warm and dry—just right!
Brush your teeth all clean and white!

Pull on your jammies, the coziest pair.
At bedtime they're the thing to wear!

Read a book, and you will see
all the things that you can be.

Find a star and make a wish:
a bike, a book—perhaps a fish!

Now pull the covers up to your chin.
Look at that—you're all tucked in!

Start at five and count to one.
Turn out the lights when you are done!

Sleep comes in every shape and way.
It's the perfect end to a perfect day.

The time has come to close your eyes.
Each dream will bring a new surprise.

Sweet "sueños"!
That means "dreams"!

Good night, sleep tight.

Now our song is at an end.
The time has come for sleep, my friend.
Let's give our hugs, and kisses too.
And then we'll say,

"Good night to you!"

Cover design © 2020 by Sourcebooks
Internal design © 2014, 2020 by Sourcebooks
Cover illustrations © Sesame Workshop
Text by Lillian Jaine
Illustrations by Marybeth Nelson

Sourcebooks and the colophon are registered trademarks of Sourcebooks.

Published by Sourcebooks Wonderland, an imprint of Sourcebooks Kids
P.O. Box 4410, Naperville, Illinois 60567–4410
(630) 961-3900
sourcebookskids.com

Originally published as *All Tucked In On Sesame Street* in 2014 in the United States of America.

Source of Production: 1010 Printing Asia Limited, North Point, Hong Kong, China
Date of Production: May 2020
Run Number: 5018734

Printed and bound in China.
OGP 10 9 8 7 6 5 4 3 2 1